THE CHALK TREE

WRITTEN BY

Melanie Masterson

ILLUSTRATED BY

Jennifer Dale Stables

To Moira, Fionnuala and Oonagh.
The colour and vibrancy of life are yours to explore.

Thanks to NuVista Energy for their
support of this project

"New house! New house! New house!" Izzy yelled.

"Rowr!" Robbie growled.

The baby kicked.

"All the houses look exactly the same,"
Dad grumbled.

"So we make it our own," Mom said,
rubbing her tummy and smiling.

Izzy's dad had a new job in a new town. So they left their small apartment in the city for a house with a yard.

But Izzy's favourite part was the brand new sidewalk. It was gleaming white, like a never-ending canvas. Her fingers itched to unpack her chalk.

"Hi folks, you must be our new neighbours."

Izzy turned to see an older couple holding a loaf of bread and a large book.

"Welcome to the neighbourhood," said the woman. "We live across the street. Here is a loaf of bread and the Community Rules."

"Community rules?" Izzy's dad asked as he was handed the heavy book.

"Sure," the man said. "Just some things the New Neighbourhood Committee agreed upon to keep our homes and streets looking perfect."

Izzy stopped listening and wandered into the house looking for her chalk amongst all the boxes.

A couple days later, chalk in hand, Izzy was finally on the sidewalk drawing. She could hear her parents talking in the background.

"What kind of tree do you think this is?" Dad asked.

"I don't know. Everyone seems to have the same tree. We should get an apple tree and plant that instead. All this space and sunshine is perfect for growing things to eat."

"Let's put the pumpkin patch over here," said Izzy's dad. Izzy's dad was passionate about pumpkins.

Robbie stalked around the yard pretending he was
a Tyrannosaurus Rex.

The baby kicked.

Izzy created.

All day long, Izzy drew and drew and drew.

She had never had such a smooth sidewalk
to work with before.

She was in heaven!

That night the doorbell rang.
Izzy was having a chalky bath. Robbie was having a fit.

Izzy's mom answered the door.

"Hello," the neighbours said with a smile. "Welcome to the neighbourhood. Here's a loaf of bread."

"That's so kind of you," said Izzy's mom.

"We also want to give you a friendly reminder that it's almost time to wash the chalk off the sidewalk."

"It's in the rule book, page 45. All sidewalk art must be washed away by 9 p.m. the same day."

"But..." Izzy's mom didn't know what to say. "What? Why?"

"To preserve the integrity of our neighbourhood of course."

Izzy's mom wanted to cry. She looked down at her big belly. The baby kicked.

"We know how busy moving must be. As a neighbourly gesture, we'll do it for you tonight."

The other neighbours agreed.

The next morning when Izzy got up she screamed. All her beautiful work was gone.

Thus the battle between the neighbours began.

Whenever Izzy drew on the sidewalk it was gone the next morning.

When Izzy's parents replaced the sad little tree on their front lawn with an apple tree the neighbours tried to stop them.

Izzy's dad dug up part of the front lawn and planted pumpkins in the middle of the night.

Sometimes, if she knew they weren't home, Izzy would draw on the neighbours' driveways just for fun. Often with the help of old Mrs. Zhang from down the street.

But later she would stand at her bedroom window and watch the neighbours washing off her work and her heart would break a little.

One day Izzy had enough. Even though her parents supported her she decided it wasn't worth it anymore.

So early one morning she got up, grabbed a little spade,
took her chalk, and buried it.
One piece of chalk on each neighbour's yard up and down the street.

As she did so she made a wish that all the grass would turn into chalk.

Afterwards she went home, got out her colouring books and crayons and didn't think about drawing on the sidewalk anymore.

The neighbours dug up the pumpkin patch one night
and laid down sod.
Izzy's parents decided it would be better to live in peace.

Winter came. The baby arrived.
Izzy and her family were happy.
It was too cold to see most of the neighbours.

One day in spring something magical
happened.

Every lawn on Izzy's street had a new tree.
A brightly coloured tree.

A chalk tree.

The neighbours didn't know what to do. There was nothing in the rule book about the spontaneous growth of trees. Some tried to cut them down but the chalky sap would spray everywhere and wouldn't wash away.

Some neighbours secretly loved the new trees. Some not so secretly.

Izzy looked out her bedroom window and smiled at the colours.

That night there was a terrible rain storm.
The wind was so bad Izzy and Robbie hid under the covers.
Even the baby was upset.

In the quiet of the morning everyone in the neighbourhood stood on their
front steps to survey the damage. All they could see was colour.
The wind had blown all the chalk off the trees, then the rain had dissolved
the chalk and deposited it everywhere.

Izzy laughed in delight.

Robbie roared.

The baby gurgled.

Kids ran out of the neighbouring houses with their own chalk in hand.

Mrs. Zhang kicked her Community Rules handbook into a pink puddle.

After that things were much more relaxed on Izzy's street.
Her dad started a pumpkin growing competition with some of the other dads.

Her mom learned how to make bread from the neighbours,
and in exchange taught them to knit.

Izzy's artwork was allowed to stay on the sidewalks.

The street never lost its colour.

Izzy smiled.

The baby giggled.

Robbie roared.

Melanie and Andrew Masterson

Melanie was raised in Calgary, Alberta and received an English degree from Concordia University in 1999. She wrote, edited and contributed to various writer communities all the way from the early days of LiveJournal to Substack. She had three daughters with her husband, Andrew, before passing away from breast cancer in December 2021.

Andrew received a PhD in Physics from the University of Calgary, and first heard a version of this (mostly true) story at work, which then inspired Melanie to write a children's story. After Melanie's passing he has edited and collaborated with various talented people to bring this project to fruition.

Jennifer Dale Stables

Jennifer is an artist, author and educator living in Okotoks, Alberta with her husband and their two children. She received a Bachelor of Fine Arts in 2001, and a Bachelor of Education in 2005 from the University of Calgary.

Through her business, Jenny Dale Designs, she creates whimsical artwork accompanied by her own poetry. Jennifer also works as an artist in residence in schools, sharing her passion for art with children and teachers. She has written and illustrated numerous picture books, and is honoured to have illustrated The Chalk Trees.

Lightning Source UK Ltd.
Milton Keynes UK
UKHW051008090223
416655UK00004B/262